W9-BII-629

Doodleville

DREW
3 YEARS OLD

5 YEARS OLD

HA HA!
DOODLES, WHERE ARE YOU GOING?

ERNESTO! I'M SO SORRY!
SORRY FOR WHAT?
YOUR DAUGHTER, SHE IS VERY TALENTED!
I...
I GUESS YOU'RE RIGHT!

7 YEARS OLD

DREW, WE LOVE HAVING YOU AT THE DINER ALL THE TIME, BUT...
DON'T YOU WANT TO GO OUT AND PLAY MORE?
DON'T YOU WANT TO MAKE FRIENDS?

I HAVE FRIENDS.
THEY'RE RIGHT HERE.

9 YEARS OLD

DREW, THAT'S FOR THE TABLES...
BUT I HAD AN IDEA!
I WANT TO DRAW HOMES FOR THE DOODLES.
A WHOLE CITY OF THEM.
WOW! WHAT WILL YOU CALL IT?

Doodl

eVILLE

CHAD SELL

ALFRED A. KNOPF NEW YORK

DREW
NOW

SWEETHEART, AREN'T YOU GOING TO BE LATE FOR SCHOOL?
NO, REMEMBER? I HAVE MY FIELD TRIP WITH ART CLUB!
OH, RIGHT! I'M SO GLAD YOU JOINED!
OF COURSE SHE DID!
SHE'S THE NEXT VAN GOGH!
VAN GOGH? YOU COULDN'T THINK OF A HAPPIER, WELL-ADJUSTED ARTIST?
ARE THERE ANY?
HA HA!
BYE, MOM!
BYE, DAD!
BYE, ERNESTO!
BYE!

WAIT!
DREW!

SHOOT.
WHAT, DID SHE FORGET SOMETHING?

NO...
I'M WORRIED ABOUT WHAT SHE MIGHT HAVE TAKEN WITH HER.

CHAPTER 1: THE ART INSTITUTE

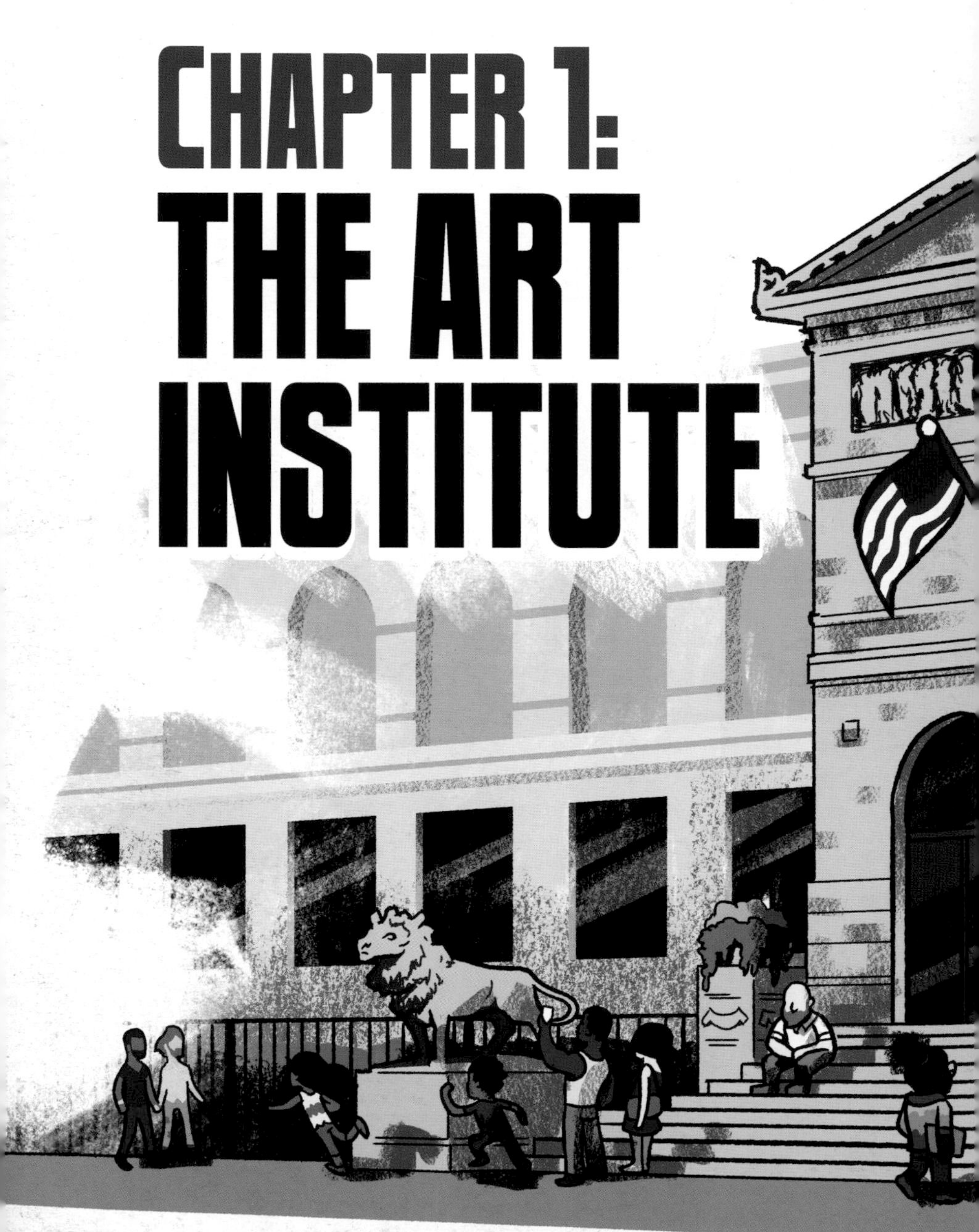

OKAY, ART CLUB!
WE'RE IN FOR A **TREAT**!
I HOPE EVERYONE BROUGHT THEIR SKETCHBOOKS!
JUST SO LONG AS YOU **ONLY** BROUGHT YOUR, UM, **BETTER-BEHAVED** CHARACTERS WITH YOU.
RIGHT?
DREW?
RIGHT!?
DREW?
WHAT? YEAH, TOTALLY!
WONDERFUL. SHALL WE HEAD IN?

HEY, MR. SCHNEIDER?
WHAT'S UP WITH THESE **LIONS**?
WHAT DO YOU MEAN, DEAR?

DO THEY **GUARD** THE MUSEUM?
ARE THEY... **DANGEROUS**?
SIGH
LIKE, WOULD THEY TEAR UP AN **ART THIEF** INTO CHUNKS?

UM, I DON'T **THINK** SO, DREW.
WHY, WERE YOU **PLANNING** SOMETHING?
HA HA! NO, OF COURSE NOT.

YEAH, SHE NEVER PLANS **ANYTHING**.
HEY!

A LITTLE WHILE LATER...
NOW, REMEMBER, I WANT EACH OF YOU TO FIND ONE PIECE THAT WILL INSPIRE YOUR NEXT PROJECT.
I'M SO EXCITED TO SEE WHAT YOU COME UP WITH!
OH, LOOK! WE CAN'T MISS DEGAS AND HIS BALLERINAS!
LET'S GO!
Great Monsters of Literature and Legends
WOWWWW...
I'VE SEEN SOME OF YOU GUYS BEFORE...
THE KRAKEN, MOBY DICK...
COOL.
WHAT'S YOUR NAME? L-E-V-I-A--
DREW! YOU'RE GOING TO MISS IT!
WHAT? BUT... ISN'T BALLET KIND OF BORING?

BUT IT'S NOT ABOUT BALLET, DREW.
IT'S ABOUT THE LIFE HE GAVE EACH AND EVERY DANCER.
THEIR GRACE, THEIR ELEGANCE!
MOST ART NEVER VENTURES OUTSIDE ITS FRAME, BUT...
ONCE THESE DANCERS GET WARMED UP, YOU JUST CAN'T STOP THEM!
AND WHY WOULD YOU?
TRULY MAGICAL, RIGHT?
HUH.

ARTISTS CAN BRING BEAUTY TO THE WORLD THAT WILL LAST LONG PAST THEIR OWN LIFETIMES.
IT'S A GIFT THAT EACH OF YOU HAS.
I HOPE YOU MAKE THE MOST OF IT.

WOW...
SO BEAUTIFUL!
AMAZING!
NOT BAD.
COOL!
NOW, KIDS, LET'S GET OUT OUR SKETCH-BOOKS!
SEE IF YOU CAN CAPTURE SOME OF THAT LIFE AND MOVEMENT IN YOUR OWN WORK.
I GUESS I'LL NEED TO START WITH A BUNCH OF TUTUS.
WHAT DO YOU THINK, DOODLES?
HUH?
OH NO!
WHAT?

SHE BROUGHT THEM!
HER DOODLES!
ALL OF THEM?
BUT MR. SCHNEIDER SAID--
WHA--?
AND THEY'RE INVADING THE ART INSTITUTE!

OH MAN, WE ARE IN SO MUCH TROUBLE.
"WE"?
WAIT, WHAT ARE THEY DOING?
UM, I DIDN'T KNOW THEY'D LIKE BALLET.
PLEASE DON'T TELL MR. SCHNEIDER.

HEY,
UM,
MR. SCHNEIDER?
YES, AMEER?
I HAVE A QUESTION.
DID I SPELL "GUSTAVE" RIGHT?
OH! LET'S SEE...
OKAY...
NOT QUITE. HERE, LET ME HELP.
NOW'S MY CHANCE...

DID ANYONE ELSE HAVE QUESTIONS?
PSST! DOODLES!
GET BACK IN HERE!
PLEASE PLEASE PLEASE??
BEFORE ANYONE SEES! C'MON!!
JUST DOWN THE HALL AND TO THE RIGHT.
OH, THANK YOU.

DREW?
YOU REALLY SHOULDN'T GET SO CLOSE TO THE WORK.
WHAT?
RIGHT.
I JUST WANTED TO GET A BETTER LOOK AT, UM...
MISTER DIGGER'S DANCERS?

RIGHT, WELL, AS I WAS SAYING...
WHAT IN THE WORLD!?
UH-OH.
DREW.
HOW MANY DOODLES GOT OUT?
THAT... IS A GOOD QUESTION.
COVER FOR ME!!

KITTYBUNNY! GET DOWN FROM THERE!
GUYS, A PILLOW FIGHT? SERIOUSLY?
DRY OFF AND CLIMB BACK IN!!

GRAB YOUR DRINKS AND GET OUTTA THERE!
PLEASE DON'T MESS ANYTHING UP, PLEEEEEEASE!!
I'M NEVER DOODLING AGAIN!!

MIKE! **THERE** YOU ARE!
I THINK YOU'RE THE **LAST ONE**!
HERE, **C'MON**.
YES, THAT BABY'S HAT IS **VERY** COOL, BUT WE'VE GOTTA GO.
EXCUSE ME, YOUNG LADY?

WHAT ARE YOU **DOING** WITH THAT ART?

OH, UH... NOTHING!
SEE, THESE ARE MY CHARACTERS, THEY'RE...
THEY GOT LOOSE.

ON THE WALLS OF THIS MUSEUM?
WHERE IS SECURITY?
THEY'RE SUPPOSED TO KEEP OUTSIDER ART FROM MEDDLING WITH THESE MASTERPIECES!

THE DOODLES WOULDN'T DO ANYTHING BAD.
EVERYTHING'S FINE.
GEEZ.
WHAT'S YOUR PROBLEM?

MY PROBLEM IS WITH ENTITLED LITTLE GIRLS WHO THINK THEIR SCRIBBLES HAVE ANY PLACE IN THE HALLS OF THIS INSTITUTE!
OKAY, I GET IT.
I'M GOING.
I'M GONE.
I LIKE DRAWING, TOO!
BYE!

DREW?

DID YOU GET THEM?
IS EVERYTHING OKAY?
WHAT HAPPENED?

CHAPTER 2: TROUBLE

I STILL CAN'T BELIEVE SHE BROUGHT THEM.
THE ART AT THAT MUSEUM IS LITERALLY PRICELESS...

SHE COULD HAVE GOTTEN IN SO. MUCH. TROUBLE.
SHE COULD HAVE GONE TO JAIL.
REALLY?

DID YOU GET INSPIRED FOR YOUR ART CLUB PROJECT, DREW?
WHAT!?
OH, I MEAN...
YEAH.
TOTALLY INSPIRED.

DID YOU DO ANY SKETCHES, OR...?
A FEW, BUT...
UMMMM...
CAN I...
SHOW YOU...
LATER?
BACK AT THE ART INSTITUTE...
WHY'S THAT BABY SO ANGRY?

WHUMP
OKAY, MY LITTLE MONSTERS...

YOU'RE HOME.

MIKE?
YOU CANNOT LET ANYONE SEE YOU WEARING THAT...
THAT BABY HAT.
I MEAN IT.
AND I AM GOING TO GET IT BACK TO THE MUSEUM, SOMEHOW.
WITHOUT... GOING TO JAIL.
AW, MIKE...

I'M NOT MAD AT YOU.
I'M NOT MAD AT ANY OF YOU.
I MADE YOU. I CAN ONLY BE MAD AT ME.
HONEY? HOW WAS YOUR FIELD TRIP?
AH!
NOTHING HAPPENED!
WHO TOLD YOU?

SORRY, DID I STARTLE YOU?
ARE YOU DOING SOMETHING WITH THE DOODLES?
UM, NO?

OKAY, YOU DON'T HAVE TO **SHOW** ME.
SHOW YOU **WHAT**?

HA HA, DREW, IT'S ALWAYS **SOMETHING**.

WAIT, DID YOU TAKE THEM TO THE **MUSEUM** TODAY?
BECAUSE THIS MORNING, I WAS **SO** WORRIED THAT--
MOM! NO, OF **COURSE** NOT.
THAT WOULD BE A **TERRIBLE** IDEA, GEEZ!

I CAN ONLY IMAGINE THE TROUBLE THEY'D GET INTO THERE.
WHAT?
WHY DOES EVERYONE ASSUME THEY'RE GONNA GET IN TROUBLE?
OH, SWEETIE, I'M SORRY.
I LOVE EVERYTHING YOU DRAW...
BECAUSE...
THEY ALWAYS DO?
EVEN IF I DON'T ALWAYS UNDERSTAND IT.
YOU HUNGRY?
TONIGHT'S SPECIAL IS MEAT LOAF!

THERE'S NOTHING SPECIAL ABOUT MEAT LOAF.
SWEETIE, I THOUGHT YOU LIKED IT!
IT'S FINE, DAD.
YOU DOING OKAY, DREW?
YEAH, ERNESTO.
I'M... OKAY.

WAIT, DID YOU DRAW **MEAT LOAF** FOR YOUR **DOODLES?**
HUH?
OH YEAH...
AMAZING.
SO, IS HE **DINNER...**
OR A NEW **FRIEND?**
HAHAHA!
HA HA, **DAD!**
I WANT TO SEE!

LATER THAT NIGHT...
DOODLES, MEET MEAT LOAF!
MEAT LOAF, THESE ARE THE REST OF THE DOODLES!
THEY HAVEN'T STOPPED DANCING SINCE WE GOT HOME FROM THE INSTITUTE.
OH! DO YOU WANT A TUTU, TOO?
HA HA, IT'S NOT A HAT, BUT...
MAYBE YOU CAN PULL IT OFF!

HEY, KIDDO!
IT'S GETTING PRETTY LATE FOR A SCHOOL NIGHT, ISN'T IT?
I GUESS SO!
THE DOODLES HAVE JUST BEEN REALLY INTO BALLET TODAY!
BALLET?
BUT ISN'T THAT... BORING?
HA HA!
GOOD NIGHT, DOODLES.
GOOD NIGHT, DREW.
NIGHT!

OKAY, DOODLES, DID EVERYONE BRUSH THEIR TEETH?

YEAH? GOOD.

WAIT, MEAT LOAF, DO YOU... **HAVE** TEETH?

NO? WELL... BE SURE TO RINSE OUT YOUR ...HOLES?

REMEMBER, EVERYONE.
MEAT LOAF IS YOUR **FRIEND**.
NOT **FOOD**.

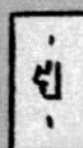
I'M LOOKING AT **YOU**, KITTYBUNNY.

IT'S BEEN...
QUITE A DAY.
LET'S HOPE THE REST OF THE WEEK ISN'T SO WILD, RIGHT?
OKAY, LOVE Y'ALL!
GOOD NIGHT!

CHAPTER 3: THE WILD WEEK

HELLO, ART CLUB! I AM SO EXCITED TO SEE YOUR SKETCHES!
I HOPE OUR FIELD TRIP GAVE YOU PLENTY OF INSPIRATION FOR YOUR NEW PROJECTS!
RIGHT... OUR... PROJECTS.
AMEER, YOU CHOSE AN IMPRESSIONIST PIECE, RIGHT?
YEAH!
I LIKED GUSTAVE CAILLEBOTTE'S PAINTING OF PARIS,
SO I WANTED TO MAKE MY OWN CITY FOR CAPTAIN COCKATOO TO KEEP SAFE FROM SUPERVILLAINS!

COOL!
SO HE'LL FLY AROUND AND DEFEAT **ALL** THE EVIL?

YEAH! **NOBODY** CAN BEAT CAPTAIN COCKATOO!
YEAH...

WHAT? YOU DON'T **THINK** SO?
I MEAN...

WHO DOES HE ACTUALLY **FIGHT**?
I HAVEN'T EVER SEEN HIM **DO** MUCH...
BESIDES **POSE** LIKE HE'S ON THE COVER OF A COMIC BOOK.

WELL, HE'S **TRAINING**! SO THAT HE'LL BE **READY**!
I JUST NEED TO COME UP WITH A **VILLAIN** FOR HIM TO FIGHT.

A...WORTHY OPPONENT!
THEN HE'LL LEAP INTO ACTION AND **TOTALLY** SAVE THE DAY!

BECK, I LOVE THIS, BUT...
I'M NOT SURE WHAT IT IS.
IT'S GOING TO BE THE SPACE-STATION HEADQUARTERS FOR DINAH DARE!
I WAS INSPIRED BY THIS COOL ABSTRACT SCULPTURE I SAW!
IT'LL BE THE HOME BASE FOR HER ADVENTURES,
AND IT'S WHERE SHE'LL STORE HER JETPACKS AND EQUIPMENT.
OOH, JETPACKS?
MY DOODLES WOULD LOVE THOSE!

IS SHE HOLDING A LASER GUN?
A PHOTON CANNON.
SHE NEEDS TO BE READY FOR ANY KIND OF EMERGENCY IN SPACE.
I'VE BEEN WORKING ON FORCE-FIELD GENERATORS,
QUARK BOMBS,
MECH ARMOR...
WHEN DOES SHE GET TO USE ALL THAT COOL STUFF?
WELL, THEY'RE JUST PROTOTYPES.
THERE'S STILL A LOT OF TESTING TO DO.
OH. RIGHT...

HOW ARE THINGS GOING FOR YOU, ZENOBIA?
GREAT!
YOU KNOW HOW THE MAGICAL BUTTERFLY BOYFRIENDS HAVE A LOT TO DEAL WITH, RIGHT?
SINCE THEY'RE BOTH PRINCES FROM TWO WARRING KINGDOMS?
YES! THE DRAMA!
WELL, I WANTED TO DO SOMETHING NICE FOR THEM, SO...
I DREW THEM THIS.

IT'S STUNNING!
WAS IT INSPIRED BY THAT LOVELY SEASCAPE AT SUNSET?
YEAH, BY FRANCIS AUGUSTUS SILVA.

ISN'T IT PRETTY? THE PRINCES GO ON A DATE THERE.
BE STILL, MY HEART!
HA HA!

WOWWWW!
I BET THE DOODLES WOULD LOVE A BEACH VACATION!

MAYBE THEY WOULD, BUT, UMM...
HOW ABOUT AFTER THE DATE?
SWOOOOON!

TJ, ARE YOU DRAWING...
A BEDROOM?
YEAH, LIKE VAN GOGH.
AH, I SEE IT NOW!
BUT... WHY?
ALL BRU WANTS IS SOME PRIVACY.
A PLACE TO BE ALONE AND STUDY MAGIC IN PEACE.
NO PARENTS, NO BROTHERS...
JUST... QUIET.

I SEE,
AND YOU...
I MEAN...
DOES BRU SHARE A BEDROOM RIGHT NOW?
YEAH, WITH A LOUD LITTLE BROTHER AND ALL HIS DUMB TOYS.
BUT YOUR BROTHER IS ADORABLE!
I LOVE RICKY!
WHAT? DREW!
I WAS TALKING ABOUT BRU.
NOT ME.
GEEZ.

DREW, YOU'VE HAD **A LOT** TO SAY ABOUT EVERYONE ELSE'S WORK,
BUT HOW IS **YOUR** PROJECT GOING?
UM...
I **DID** TEACH MY DOODLES SOME COOL DANCE MOVES AFTER THEY MET THOSE...
I MEAN, I **TOLD** THEM ALL ABOUT THE BALLET DANCERS AT THE INSTITUTE.
YEAH.
...AND I DREW THEM SOME CUTE TUTUS?
I, UH...
I WAS **REALLY** HOPING YOU WOULD HAVE MORE TO **SHOW** TODAY, DREW.

WELL, I ALSO MADE ANOTHER DOODLE NAMED **MEAT LOAF** LAST NIGHT...
BECAUSE... MY DAD MAKES THIS MEAT LOAF THAT I...
UM, HE'S IN HERE **SOMEWHERE**...
WAIT, WHERE DID EVERYBODY **GO**!??
OH.
WHOOPS.

HEY!
COME BACK
AND CLEAN UP
MY ROOM!
MY
EQUIPMENT!!
MY
BEAUTIFUL
BEACH!!

DOODLES, DON'T HURT YOURSELVES!!
DON'T HURT ANYTHING!
CAPTAIN COCKATOO!

I GUESS DINAH DARE GOT A CHANCE TO TEST THAT FORCE FIELD, HUH, BECK?

SO...THAT'S GOOD, RIGHT?

STUPENDOUS.

AHEM.
OH! IS BRU OKAY, TJ?
THEY WILL BE ONCE THEY GET THAT HAT BACK.
SORRY ABOUT THAT!
HE JUST LOVES HATS. I DON'T KNOW WHY.
HEY, ZENOBIA.
HI.
I'M SORRY YOUR BEACH GOT MESSED UP.
IT'S OKAY.

LATER...
YOU DO BELONG IN ART CLUB, DREW.
BUT THE DOODLES DON'T MAKE IT EASY, DO THEY?
NOTHING'S EASY WITH THEM.
THEY NEVER DO WHAT I TELL THEM.
THEY JUST LOVE TO EXPLORE AND...
DANCE?
EVERYONE ELSE IN ART CLUB HAS CHARACTERS THAT ARE SO COOL AND COMPLICATED...
AND WELL BEHAVED.
MINE LOOK LIKE SOMETHING A LITTLE KID WOULD DRAW.
SURE, YOUR DOODLES ARE SIMPLE, BUT THEY'VE GOT TONS OF PERSONALITY.
MR. SCHNEIDER JUST WANTS YOU TO CHALLENGE YOURSELF, TO THINK BIG.
HMM...

YOU KNOW, I LIKE THE SOUND OF THAT.
SOMETHING BIG!
SOMETHING AMAZING!
YEAH...IT'LL BE INCREDIBLE! MWAHAHAHA!
I'LL SHOW THEM!
UM...
I DON'T THINK YOU SHOULD GET CARRIED AWAY...
THANKS, ZENOBIA!!
DREW?
SEE YOU AT SCHOOL TOMORROW!
SIGH...

WOW!
RICKY, LEAVE DREW ALONE. SHE'S **BUSY**.
HA HA, IT'S OKAY! I THINK I'M DONE!
HE'S SO BIG! AND...SCARY!
YEAH? **RIGHT**??
IS HE... A **MONSTER**?

YEAH, HIS NAME IS... THE LEVERATHON!
THAT'S KIND OF A WEIRD NAME.
YEAH, I DON'T THINK I GOT IT RIGHT.
I WROTE IT DOWN. THE... L-E-V-I-A-T-H-A-N.
WHAT DOES HE EAT?
OOOH, ANYTHING HE WANTS! SUPERHEROES! SPACE ADVENTURERS! HE'LL EAT THEM ALL!
I MEAN, HE COULD. BUT...HE WON'T. IF THEY'RE NICE.
HA HA! HELLO, MR. LEVITATION!
LET'S JUST CALL HIM LEVI, OKAY?

THAT NIGHT...
DOODLES, I MADE A NEW FRIEND!
WHAT DO YOU THINK OF HIM?
AW, RONNIE, LEVI DOESN'T MAKE **YOUR** MUSCLES ANY LESS IMPRESSIVE.
BUT HIS **TEETH** ARE PRETTY COOL, RIGHT, GLOOP?
HA HA! KITTYBUNNY, I DOUBT HE EVEN **FEELS** THAT!

DOODLES! DO YOU EXPECT HIM TO GIVE YOU A **RIDE**?
HE'S NOT A **BUS**!
HE--

CHAPTER 4: THE LEVIATHAN

I CALL HIM...
LEVI!
WELL, HE IS... BIG!
IS HE SUPPOSED TO LOOK SO... GOOFY?
YEAH, IS HE SUPPOSED TO BE SILLY OR SCARY?
HE'S NOT VERY MENACING FOR A MONSTER.
MAYBE IF YOU DREW HIM EATING SOMETHING?
OR SOMEONE?
YEAH!
RAISE THE STAKES!
BUT... THAT'S NOT REALLY WHAT I...
THAT'S NOT LEVI.
WELL, IT WAS A GOOD EFFORT, DREW.
WHO WANTS TO GO NEXT?

SO... THIS IS BIRD CITY, WHERE CAPTAIN COCKATOO LIVES.
I'M NOT GOOD AT DRAWING BUILDINGS, BUT I **THINK** THEY LOOK OKAY?
I TRIED TO TEACH MYSELF HOW TO DO PERSPECTIVE, BECAUSE I HAD
GOOFY
SILLY
MENACING
MONSTER
UM, WHAT? **DUDE.**

OH! LEVI!! GET OUT OF BIRD CITY!
SORRY, HE JUST LIKES TO EXPLORE AND...
RR?
HEY! THAT SKYSCRAPER ISN'T A SNACK!
CAPTAIN COCKATOO! DEFEND YOUR CITY!!

STOP! DON'T!
YOU'RE HURTING HIM!
THIS IS AMAZING!
STOP!!
LEVI DIDN'T MEAN TO...
HE...
RARGHHHHH!!

DINAH, HELP HIM OUT!
KIDS, CALM DOWN! THIS...
STOP! **STOP!!**
GET HIM, BRU!
DREW, HE'S HURTING HIM! CAN'T YOU **DO** SOMETHING?
STOP!
DREW!
DREW!
STOP!
DREW! STOP HIM!
DREW!!
DREW!!!
STOP!!!
HE'S GONNA **EAT** CAPTAIN COCKATOO!!
DREW!
HURRY!
YOU HAVE TO **DO**
HE'S NOT GONNA **MAKE**

I SAID STOP!!!

HE'S...
HE'S STILL GOT HIM!
WHAT!?
NO!
LEVI!
I'M SORRY! I'M SORRY! I'M SORRY!

DEAR, ARE YOU OKAY?
I'M SORRY, DREW. I DIDN'T...
DREW?

DREW! WAIT!
ARE YOU OKAY?

IS SHE GONNA BE...?
KIDS, LET'S...
GIVE HER SOME SPACE.

RARGHHH!

CHAPTER 5: THE DARK LEVIATHAN

LEVI!

ARE YOU OUT THERE?

LEEEEEEVIIIIII!!!

I'M SORRY.

...IT WASN'T YOUR **FAULT**.

HUH?
LEVI!
HA HA!
I **KNEW** YOU'D COME BACK!
I'M SORRY! I HOPE...

RARRGHH!

WHAT??
LEVI?

IS THAT...
YOU?

RARGGH

NO!
LEVI!

THE NEXT MORNING...
HEY!
ZEN!
HEY, AMEER.
HOW ARE YOU?
HOW'S... CAPTAIN COCKATOO?

OH, YOU KNOW...
HE'LL BE FINE.
BUT...
HAVE YOU HEARD FROM DREW?
IS SHE OKAY?
I DON'T KNOW.
YESTERDAY...
THAT WAS AWFUL.
I...
WAAAAIT.

HE'S... DIFFERENT.
HE'S ANGRY.
I TRIED TO TALK TO HIM, BUT...
WHAT? WHO?
YEAH, WHAT'S GOING ON?
IT'S... THE...
THE LEVIATHAN! HE'S GONE!
WHAT? WHERE DID HE GO!?

HE...
HE CAME TO ME.

ARE WE SAFE?
COULD HE COME HERE!?
AMEER, CALM DOWN, GEEZ.
HE'S A TWO-DIMENSIONAL DRAWING.
HE CAN'T HURT ANY OF US.
HE COULDN'T HURT ME, BUT...
BUT WHAT?
HE...
THE...
OH NO.
DREW...

...HE DESTROYED DOODLEVILLE.

HE WAS AFTER THE DOODLES.
THEY STAYED HIDDEN UNTIL HE WENT AWAY.
OH, DREW...
BUT BY THEN, THE WHOLE CITY WAS IN PIECES.
THAT MONSTER DID ALL THIS?
HMMM.

MAYBE IT'S NOT AS BAD AS IT LOOKS?
ARE YOU KIDDING ME?
I AM FREAKING OUT RIGHT NOW.

LET'S HAVE DINAH EVALUATE THESE BUILDINGS.
SOME OF THE STRUCTURES MIGHT STILL BE INTACT.
WE CAN HELP YOU REBUILD, DREW!
BETTER THAN EVER!
BUT...
WHAT'S THE POINT IF HE'S STILL OUT THERE?
THE DOODLES WON'T BE SAFE.
MY PRINCES CAN HELP DEFEND THEM!
YEAH, DREW!
BRU'S BEEN STUDYING SOME SICK NEW SPELLS.
HEY, AMEER!
SUPERHEROES LOVE TEAM-UPS, RIGHT?
UM, I MEAN...
THEY DO.

GUYS, YOU DON'T UNDERSTAND.
HE'S TOO POWERFUL...
TOO DANGEROUS.
DREW, WE'VE GOT MAGIC AND SCIENCE AND SUPERHEROES!
TOGETHER, WE'RE UNSTOPPABLE!
RIGHT, AMEER?
RIGHT. YEAH!
ART CLUB UNITED!!

BUT...

BUT IF ANY OF THEM GET **HURT**, I DON'T...
IT WOULD BE ALL MY FAULT.
DREW, STOP...
ALL OF THIS, IT'S...
...IT'S ALL MY FAULT!
DREW!
SERIOUSLY! **STOP!!!!**

RARGHHH!!!
WHAT IS EVEN HAPPENING?!
HE CAME OUT OF NOWHERE!
HE'S ENORMOUS!

HE...

I...

OH NO.

NO NO
NO NO
NO!!!!!!!

CAPTAIN, DON'T BE A HERO!
STAY AWAY FROM THAT THING!
AMEER, CALM DOWN, HE'LL BE...
FINE?

CAPTAIN, DON'T BE A HERO!
STAY AWAY FROM THAT THING!
AMEER, CALM DOWN, HE'LL BE...
FINE?

I **TOLD** YOU THE PRINCES WOULD DEFEND DOODLEVILLE!
WHEN THEY LINK THEIR MAGIC, THEY'RE **UNBEATABLE**!

ZEN, I...

EVERYONE, GET YOUR CHARACTERS, GRAB **AS MANY** DOODLES AS YOU **CAN**...
HUH?

AND PLEASE JUST GET FAR AWAY FROM HERE.
BUT...
PLEASE.

SHE'S **RIGHT**, WE NEED TO **EVACUATE**!
IT'S A LOST CAUSE!

HURRY!
KIDS?
KEEP THEM SAFE FOR ME!!!
WHAT IS GOING ON HERE?

RIIIIPPP

I'M SORRY.
I'M SORRY.
DREW?
ARE YOU OKAY?
...NO.

THIS...
IS THIS...
THE LEVIATHAN?
HE WAS.
THEN...
HE CHANGED.
I...
I THINK HE'S STILL ALIVE.

GRRRRRRRRRRRRRRRRRRRF
SSSSSSSSSSSSH

DREW!!
STOP!
WHAT ARE YOU DOING??
STOP!
PLEASE, STOP!!!

CHAPTER 6:
IN PIECES

DREW?
SWEETHEART?

I DON'T WANT TO TALK ABOUT IT.

BUT, DREW...
WE'RE WORRIED ABOUT YOU.

YOU CAN TALK TO US ABOUT... WHATEVER THIS IS.
YOU'RE NOT EATING...
NOT TALKING...

AND...
WHERE ARE ALL YOUR DOODLES?

DOODLEVILLE IS TORN UP ON THE FLOOR...

HE'S HUNTING THEM.
THE LEVIATHAN.
HE'S TRYING TO DESTROY THEM.
YOUR ART PROJECT IS AFTER THE DOODLES?
ARE THEY SAFE?
THEY'RE WITH ART CLUB.
THE DOODLES ARE SAFER WITH THEM.
AND FAR AWAY FROM ME.
OH, DARLING...
I DON'T KNOW HOW IT ALL WENT WRONG.
I JUST WANTED TO MAKE SOMETHING BIGGER AND BETTER THAN I EVER HAD BEFORE.
I THOUGHT THAT WAS THE POINT.

SWEETHEART, IT'S NOT YOUR FAULT.
BUT IT IS.
I MADE THAT MONSTER, AND NOW NOTHING CAN STOP HIM.
IT'S MY FAULT HE DESTROYED DOODLEVILLE,
AND IT'S MY FAULT THAT HE...
THAT...
DREW? WHAT DID HE DO?
HE KILLED ZENOBIA'S BUTTERFLY PRINCE...
AND I DON'T KNOW IF SHE'LL EVER FORGIVE ME.

WELL...

YOU CAN FIND OUT SOON, BECAUSE...
SHE'S DOWNSTAIRS IN THE DINER.
WHAT?!?
SHE'S HERE?

BUT...
I CAN'T.
I DON'T...
I DON'T EVEN KNOW WHAT TO SAY.

I THINK YOU KNOW WHERE TO START.

BUT...

ZEN, I'M...
I'M SO SORRY.
DREW!

WHY ARE YOU SORRY?
BECAUSE...
IT'S MY FAULT YOUR PRINCE IS DEAD.

DREW, IT'S NOT YOUR FAULT.
AND HE'S NOT DEAD.

BUT...
YOU WERE THERE.
YOU SAW WHAT HAPPENED.
THE PRINCES ARE MAGICALLY LINKED.
IF ONE DIES, THE OTHER WILL KNOW.
HE'S STILL INSIDE THAT THING...
AND WE'RE GONNA GET HIM BACK.
WHAT? WHO IS?
YOU, ME, OUR FRIENDS.
THE DOODLES. EVERYONE.
IT'S TOO DANGEROUS, ZEN.
WE CAN'T BEAT THE LEVIATHAN.
I THINK YOU'RE WRONG, DREW.
BECAUSE TOGETHER...
I THINK WE CAN DO JUST ABOUT ANYTHING.

LATER...
SO, UM...
HAS ANYONE HEARD FROM DREW?
NO.
SIGH...
HOW ARE HER DOODLES?
THEY'RE REALLY SAD.
AND SCARED.
I JUST FEEL SO BAD FOR THEM.
THEY MISS HER.

GREAT! YOU'RE ALL **HERE**!
HUH?
WHAT'S GOING ON?
YEAH, WHY ARE YOU SO... **HAPPY**?
BECAUSE ZENOBIA, SHE...
CAN YOU **SHOW** THEM?
HA HA, SURE.

ZEN TAUGHT THE DOODLES HER BUTTERFLY MAGIC!

AND THEY CAN **LINK** THEIR MAGIC TOGETHER!
AMAZING, RIGHT?

IF SHE COULD DO **THAT**, THEN...
MAYBE ALL OF **YOU** CAN TRAIN THE DOODLES TO BE HEROES, TOO!

AND THEN MAYBE...
WE COULD DEFEAT THE DARK LEVIATHAN?
MAYBE?
UM.
WHY AREN'T ANY OF YOU SAYING ANYTHING?
BECAUSE THAT IS THE COOLEST IDEA I'VE EVER HEARD!
LIKE, AN ENTIRE DOODLE ARMY??
AN ARMY OF SUPERDOODLES!

I HAVE SO MANY IDEAS!
THEY'LL BE UNSTOPPABLE!
THEY'LL DESTROY THE LEVIATHAN!
GIANT NEW PROJECTS!
VEHICLES!
WEAPONRY!
WAIT!
STOP!
WE CAN'T DO THAT HERE.
NOT NOW.
WITH ALL THE DOODLES TOGETHER...
THEY'RE TOO MUCH OF A TARGET.

BUT...
WE HAVE TO WORK TOGETHER, RIGHT?
IT'S, LIKE, THE ENTIRE POINT OF THE PLAN.

RIGHT.
BUT NOT UNTIL WE'RE READY TO FACE THE LEVIATHAN AGAIN.

UNTIL THEN... WE HAVE TO KEEP THE DOODLES SAFE.
YOU HAVE TO KEEP THEM SAFE.

SO, UM...
WHO'S FREE AFTER SCHOOL?

CHAPTER 7: SUPERDOODLES

COME ON IN!
DAAAD, I'M HOME!
AMEER, YOUR PLACE IS SO--
WHAT IS THAT?!

AMEER, DUCK!!

HA HA, HE'S NOT A DUCK, DREW.
ARE YA?
WAIT.
IS THAT...
A COCKATOO?
HE'S SO BIG!
AND PINK!
HELLO! HELLO!
AND HE TALKS?
YEAH, HE'S PRETTY GREAT.
WAIT, WAIT...
LET ME GUESS...
IS HIS NAME... CAPTAIN?

SO WHERE SHOULD WE START?
SUPER-POWERS?
SECRET IDENTITIES?
COOL COSTUMES?
HA HA, WELL...
WE SHOULD FIGURE OUT WHAT PART EACH DOODLE WILL PLAY ON THE TEAM.
LIKE RONNIE HERE, HE'LL BE THE BIG, BRAWNY DUDE.
DOES THIS DO THE TRICK?
WOW!!
HE LOOKS AMAZING!!
HA HA!

I THINK MO WANTS TO GO NEXT!
HE'LL BE THE FUNNY, FAST ONE ON THE TEAM.
JUMPING AROUND AND USING HIS AGILITY RATHER THAN HIS MUSCLES.
AWWW!
BUT I THINK HE REALLY WANTS SOME MUSCLES!
CAN YOU ADD SOME TO HIS COSTUME?
PERFECT!

SO, DOODLES,
HOW ARE YOU FEELING?
WELL, THEY SEEM CONFIDENT, BUT...
DO YOU REALLY THINK WE'LL HAVE A CHANCE AGAINST THAT...
THE DARK LEVIATHAN?
OF COURSE!
LOOK AT EVERYTHING YOU'VE DONE WITH THE DOODLES ALREADY!
THEY'RE GOING TO BE AMAZING!
I HOPE SO.
I DON'T KNOW WHAT I'LL DO WHEN I SEE THAT THING AGAIN.
WELL, IT'S LIKE YOU SAID...
EVERY HERO NEEDS A "WORTHY OPPONENT," RIGHT?
I THINK YOU'VE FOUND HIM.

LATER...
ARE YOU SURE YOU DON'T WANT TO TAKE THE DOODLES HOME WITH YOU?
I WISH I COULD, BUT...
THEY NEED YOU TO TRAIN THEM, AMEER.
AND KEEP THEM SAFE.
WELL...
CAN I AT LEAST WALK YOU HOME?
HA HA, AMEER, YOU DON'T HAVE TO!
BUT... I WANT TO.

WHAT ARE YOU DOING HERE?
THEY'RE GONE! THERE'S NOTHING LEFT FOR YOU!
GO!!
AND DON'T COME BACK!
DON'T YOU DARE!!

CHAPTER 8: EVIL BAD SCARY STUFF

HI, MOM.
HI, DAD.
GOOD MORNING, SWEETHEART!
GOOD MORNING, DREW!
DREEEW!
HEY, DREW.
HI--
TJ?

WHAT ARE **YOU** DOING HERE?

I CAME WITH ABUELO ERNESTO SO THAT I COULD SHOW YOU SOMETHING.
IS THAT COOL?
OH, SURE...

WANNA GRAB A BOOTH AND...?
SURE.

HERE, UM...

HEY.
ARE YOU... OKAY?

YEAH, I JUST...
DIDN'T SLEEP WELL.

ARE YOU **SURE** YOU'RE OKAY?

I MEAN...
I'M HAPPY THAT EVERYONE IN ART CLUB IS **HELPING** BUT...

I JUST... I MISS THE **DOODLES,** AND...
I WISH THEY WERE **SAFE** WITH **ME**.

I JUST FEEL LIKE EVERYTHING I DO IS A **DISASTER**.

I KNOW IT MIGHT **FEEL** LIKE THAT,
BUT WE'RE **HERE** FOR YOU. WE'LL FIGURE IT OUT.
THANKS.
YOU'RE BEING NICE.
I SORT OF THOUGHT YOU **HATED** ME.

BUT I GUESS I'VE BEEN HARD ON YOU.
I'M SORRY.
I DIDN'T **GET** WHAT YOU WERE DOING WITH THE DOODLES.

OOOOH!
ARE YOU TEACHING THEM MAGIC?
BLACK MAGIC?
EVIL BAD SCARY STUFF?

YOU'RE NOT A WITCH, ARE YOU?
HAHAHA!
WOULD YOU TELL ME IF YOU WERE??

I'M NOT A WITCH.
I JUST LIKE THAT KINDA STUFF.

WITCHCRAFT?
CURSES AND INCANTATIONS?
NOT EXACTLY...

MORE LIKE... THE IDEA.
THAT BEING DIFFERENT CAN MAKE YOU POWERFUL.

YOU'VE GOT TO **MAKE PEACE** WITH YOUR DEMONS, OR THEY'LL SWALLOW YOU WHOLE.

SO YOU'RE SAYING THE DARK LEVIATHAN IS PART OF ME?
OF COURSE. YOU MADE HIM.

I THINK IT HAPPENS TO A LOT OF ARTISTS, DREW.
THE ART INSTITUTE IS FULL OF DARK AND SCARY STUFF.
REALLY?
YEAH, THERE'S A LOT THERE THAT WE DIDN'T SEE.

YOU SHOULD GO BACK!
MAYBE YOU COULD LEARN SOMETHING.

IT'S TIME FOR SCHOOL, KIDS.
READY TO GO?
YAYYYY!

ACTUALLY, I NEED TO...
CHECK ON SOMETHING.
BYEEE!
SEE YOU, DREW!

HMMM...

UM, DAD?
HOW WOULD YOU FEEL ABOUT...
A FIELD TRIP?

SO...THIS MONSTER...
THE...DARK LEVIATHAN?
YOU THINK HE APPEARS WHENEVER...
WHENEVER I'M FEELING REALLY BAD.
BUT...
WHAT MAKES YOU FEEL SO TERRIBLE?
DAD...
I DUNNO.
LOTS OF STUFF.
NOTHING I DO TURNS OUT RIGHT.
IT'S COMPLICATED.

I'M SO SORRY, SWEETHEART.
I WISH I COULD DO MORE TO HELP.
THANKS, DAD.

WELL, UM...
I THINK "DARK AND SCARY" IS RIGHT.
THIS ARTIST WAS DEFINITELY, UM, WORKING THROUGH A LOT OF ISSUES.
YEAH...
IT'S LIKE HE PAINTED EVERY DARK, GROSS FEELING HE EVER HAD.
WHY WOULD HE DO THAT?
WELL...
MAYBE IT HELPED HIM?
TO UNDERSTAND WHAT HE WAS THINKING AND FEELING?
LIKE YOU SAID, IT CAN BE... COMPLICATED.

YOU SHOULDN'T BE ANYWHERE NEAR THAT PAINTING, YOU THIEF!
YOU??
WHAT, DO YOU LIVE HERE?
I AM ON THE BOARD OF DIRECTORS!
WHICH HAS BEEN IN CHAOS SINCE YOU DEFACED THAT PORTRAIT!
WHAT ARE YOU TALKING ABOUT? THE BABY?
I DIDN'T TAKE ITS FACE,
I TOOK THE HAT!
I MEAN, NO I DIDN'T.
AHA!
I KNEW IT!
IT WAS AN ACCIDENT!

I DON'T KNOW WHAT HAT YOU'RE TALKING ABOUT,
BUT YOU CAN'T SPEAK TO MY DAUGHTER LIKE THAT.
SHE JUST CONFESSED!
TO WHAT?
SHE WOULDN'T--
TELL HIM, TELL HIM WHAT YOU DID!
DREW...?
WHAT IS SHE EVEN...
DREW?

DONUTS!!!
WHAT? DAD!!
LET'S GO GET SOME!
RIGHT NOW!
STAN'S? DO-RITE?
WHICHEVER YOU WANT!
BOTH!
DAAAAAAD!!!
WHAT ARE YOU DOING?
DASHING FOR DONUTS!

WHAT IN THE WORLD IS GOING ON?
ROARRR
NOW WHAT?!?
GRRRGHHH!
RARGHH!

WOW.

BUT...

ARE YOU **HUNGRY**?

BECAUSE I WAS **SERIOUS** ABOUT THOSE DONUTS.

THAT NIGHT...

RR

LEVIATHAN?
IS THAT YOU?

GRRRRR...
SHHH, IT'S OKAY.

HERE.
I DREW YOU SOMETHING.

SNFF SNFF
YOU'RE... SUSPICIOUS?
IT'S NOT POISONED.
I...
I WOULDN'T DO THAT.
YOU KEEP COMING BACK HERE.
ARE YOU LONELY?
HUNGRY?
SEE? IT'S GOOD, HUH?
MAYBE WE CAN START OVER,
LEARN TO TRUST EACH OTHER AGAIN?
DREW?
AH!
ARE YOU UP?
IT'S THE MIDDLE OF THE NIGHT!

NO! I MEAN...
I'M GOING RIGHT BACK TO BED!
WELL, OKAY.
LEVIATHAN?
DID YOU WANT ANOTHER DONUT?
SEE YOU LATER, I GUESS.

THE NEXT DAY...
SO I HAVE THIS IDEA WHERE THEY FOCUS THEIR MAGIC AND...
THEN...
DREW? IS SOMETHING BOTHERING YOU?
I WAS...
I WAS JUST THINKING ABOUT THE LEVIATHAN.
DON'T WORRY ABOUT HIM, DREW.
OUR PLAN WILL WORK.

NO, I WAS THINKING ABOUT HOW HE **WAS**, AT FIRST.
WHAT DO YOU MEAN?

HE WAS... **SWEET**.
HE ONLY **ACTED** BAD BECAUSE I WAS **FEELING** BAD.

WE DON'T **BLAME** YOU, DREW.
WE'LL HELP YOU **STOP** HIM.

BUT...
WHAT IF I COULD **SAVE** HIM INSTEAD?

DREW...

THE **PLAN** IS TO DEFEND THE DOODLES AND **SAVE** THE BUTTERFLY PRINCE.
NOT THE MONSTER YOU MADE.

BUT...
HE'S A **PART** OF ME!

A PART OF YOU THAT WANTED TO **DESTROY** DOODLEVILLE AND EVERYONE IN IT?

THAT'S NOT FAIR.
I'M SORRY, BUT IT'S **TRUE**!

I'VE GOTTA GO.

DREW, I JUST...
I DON'T WANT YOU TO...
...TO DO SOMETHING **STUPID**?

WELL...
TOO LATE.

THAT NIGHT...

HOW ARE YOU, SWEETIE?
ARE YOU **HUNGRY**?
NO...
THEN WHY ARE YOU **DRAWING** SO MUCH FOOD?
IT'S...FOR THE LEVIATHAN.
OH.

I'M...
I WANT TO UNDERSTAND HIM.
MAYBE EVEN **MAKE PEACE** WITH HIM.

ARE YOU... **SURE** THAT'S **POSSIBLE**?
NOT AT ALL.

CHAPTER 9: FEEDING THE BEAST

YOU LIKE IT, HUH?
I GUESS GROWING UP IN A DINER IS GOOD FOR SOMETHING.
THAT'S EVERYTHING I DREW, DUDE.
YOU'RE STILL HUNGRY?
I COULD DRAW SOME MORE, BUT...
YOU'RE GETTING SO BIG!
GRRR
HEY, THAT'S ENOUGH.
RRARGHHH!!!

I'M TRYING TO HELP YOU!
DON'T YOU GET THAT?
AND YOU KEEP TREATING ME LIKE I'M THE MONSTER!
HOW MANY TIMES DO I HAVE TO SAY I'M SORRY?

THE NEXT MORNING...

HEY, BECK.
OH! HI!
UM...
THIS IS... A **LOT**.
WE HAVE TO BE **READY** FOR **EVERY** SCENARIO, DREW.

HI, DOODLES!
HAVE YOU BEEN HELPING BECK WITH HER GIANT ROBOTS AND LASERS AND...
WHATEVER THOSE ARE?
THEY'VE ACTUALLY BEEN QUITE CAPABLE LAB ASSISTANTS!
COOL!
AND THOSE ARE CONTAINMENT-FIELD GENERATORS.
OH.

I THINK SO... LIKE WHEN I'M FEELING REALLY BAD.

INTERESTING. BUT NOT EXACTLY RELIABLE.

DONUTS?
AND LOTS OF THINGS.
PRETTY MUCH ANYTHING.

BUT...
WHERE DOES HE FIND DONUTS?
UMM...
...OR DRAWINGS OF DONUTS?

HAVE YOU BEEN FEEDING HIM, DREW!?
SHHHH!!

I MEAN...

I'VE BEEN MAKING PROGRESS WITH HIM...
DREW!!

WHY DOESN'T ANYONE WANT TO GIVE HIM A CHANCE?
IF YOU FEED HIM, HE'LL ONLY GET STRONGER!
AND BIGGER!
HAS HE GOTTEN EVEN BIGGER?
UM...
I CAN'T BELIEVE YOU WOULD DO THAT, DREW!
ACTUALLY, MAYBE I CAN.
KIDS, IF YOU CAN'T BE QUIET, YOU'LL NEED TO...
THAT'S NOT FAIR! JUST LISTEN...
I'VE HEARD ENOUGH!
FINE!
I DON'T NEED YOUR HELP, ANYWAY!

DID SHE EVEN CHECK OUT THOSE BOOKS?

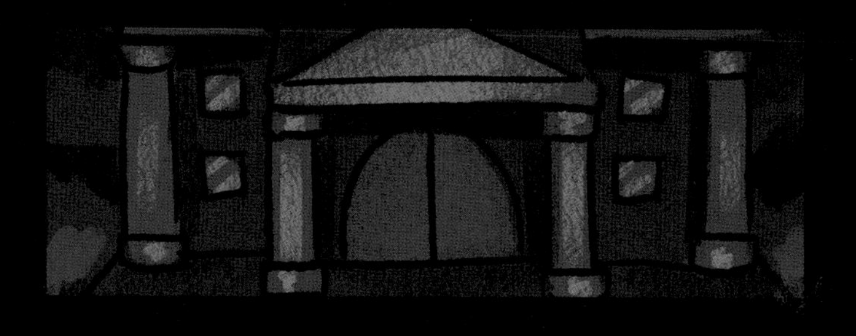

UM...

SO... THIS IS WEIRD.

HOW AM I HERE?
IS THIS ANOTHER MESSED-UP NIGHTMARE?
WHERE IS EVERYBODY?
DOODLES!
WHERE ARE YOU?
AHHH!

LEVI!
YOU'RE... **YOU**!

HA HA, I'M SO GLAD TO **SEE** YOU!!

HEY, LET'S GO FIND THE **DOODLES**!
AND THEN...

AND...

LEVI, RUN!
HOW MANY ARE THERE?
WHY ARE THEY DOING THIS?
AAHH!
NO!
LEVI!

WHO ARE YOU?
WHAT DO YOU WANT?
HELP ME, PLEASE!
HELP LEVI!
HELP!

AAHHH!!

SWEETIE?
YOU LOOK AWFUL.
THANKS, MOM.

DID YOU FORGET YOUR BREAKFAST PLANS?
PLANS?

YOU KNOW, WITH YOUR FRIENDS?
FRIENDS? WHAT FRIENDS?

GOOD, SHE'S UP!

LOOKS LIKE YOU CAN START YOUR MEETING, KIDS!

CHAPTER 10: ART CLUB UNITED?

SO...

I KNOW WHY YOU'RE HERE.
DREW...
LET ME SAY SOMETHING FIRST.

I HAVEN'T GIVEN YOU MUCH OF A REASON TO TRUST ME, BUT...
I WAS JUST TRYING TO MAKE THINGS RIGHT.

BECK TOLD US EVERYTHING, DREW.
IS IT TRUE?

LEVI...HE SHOULDN'T SUFFER FOR WHAT I DID.
I TRIED TO CROSS HIM OUT LIKE HE WAS JUST...SOME KIND OF MISTAKE.

BUT...
WHY HAVE YOU BEEN FEEDING HIM, DREW?
HOW BIG HAS HE GOTTEN?
I WANTED TO SHOW HIM THAT I...
THAT HE'S NOT A MISTAKE.
BUT MAYBE I JUST MADE EVERYTHING WORSE.
I SHOULDN'T HAVE TRIED TO FIX EVERYTHING ON MY OWN.
I SHOULD HAVE TOLD YOU.
I REALLY LIKED BEING YOUR FRIEND.
I REALLY LIKED BEING IN ART CLUB.
I JUST WANTED TO SAY SORRY. FOR EVERYTHING.
DREW... GEEZ...
DO YOU THINK WE'RE HERE TO KICK YOU OUT OF ART CLUB?
...UM...

WE'RE HERE TO HELP YOU, DREW.
TO TRY YOUR PLAN.
YOUR DOODLES ARE READY.
WE'RE READY.
THE DOODLES?
ALL OF THEM?
YOU BROUGHT ALL OF THEM HERE?
ART CLUB UNITED!
ART CLUB UNITED!
ART CLUB UNITED.
ART CLUB UNITED!

BUT...
BUT I DON'T EVEN KNOW WHERE TO START!
YOU HAVE A PLAN, RIGHT?
LET'S START WITH THAT!
I...
THE DOODLES, THEY'RE NOT SAFE HERE...
YOU HAVE TO...
CALM DOWN, DREW. WE'LL FIGURE SOMETHING OUT!
BUT...
THERE'S NO TIME!

NO NO NO
NO NO
NO!
DREW?
WHERE ARE YOU GOING, SWEETIE?
IS EVERYTHING OKAY?

NO.

NOT AT ALL.

RRRAA

AGHHH

HE'S HUGE!
DREW, WHAT HAVE YOU BEEN FEEDING HIM?
WE CAN'T FIGHT THAT!
WAIT! WAIT!
WE HAVE TO! WE ARE READY!
I'LL HOLD HIM OFF FOR AS LONG AS YOU NEED!

IT'S TIME TO SAVE THE DAY, COCKATOO COMMANDOS!

BAM
POW!
PUNCH!
YEAH!
JUST LIKE WE PRACTICED!
NOW GO FOR HIS **TAIL**!

RRRAR?
THAT'S IT!!!
SLAM!!

QUICK!
SCATTER BEFORE HE...
WAIT, WHY...
WHAT'S...?
WHAT'S HAPPENING!?

THEY'RE STUCK TO HIM!
HE'S...
HE'S ABSORBING THEM!
THEY'RE... THEY...
MY COMMANDOS!
I...
WHAT CAN WE DO?
AMEER, I'M SO SORRY...

DON'T WORRY, DREW!
WE'RE JUST GETTING STARTED!
HUH?
IT'S TIME, DOODLES!
TIME FOR TEAM MAGIC!

BUTTERFLY BRIGADE,
YOU'RE UP FIRST!!
SHINE **BRIGHT,** BRIGADE!!

RRP?

WHAT DID THEY JUST DO?
ZENOBIA?
WHAT'S GOING ON?
PLEASE WORK, PLEASE...

RRARGHHHHHH

THEY FOUND HIM!
THE BUTTERFLY BOYFRIENDS ARE BACK TOGETHER!!
THAT'S AMAZING, ZEN!!
AFTER ALL THIS TIME!
THEY'RE SOOOO BEAUTIFUL!
NOW IT'S MY TURN.

GO FORTH, MY COVEN!!
IT'S THE WITCHING HOUR!!

QUICKLY! WHILE THE BUTTERFLY BRIGADE IS STILL FIGHTING!
USE THE SPELLS I TAUGHT YOU!
GATHER UP THE DARKNESS!
USE IT!
MASTER IT!

RICKY'S RIGHT!

HE'S IN **AGONY**!

YOU'RE TEARING HIM APART!

RAPPPPPP

RNNFF

THIS... IT'S NOT GONNA...
NONE OF THIS IS **WORKING.**

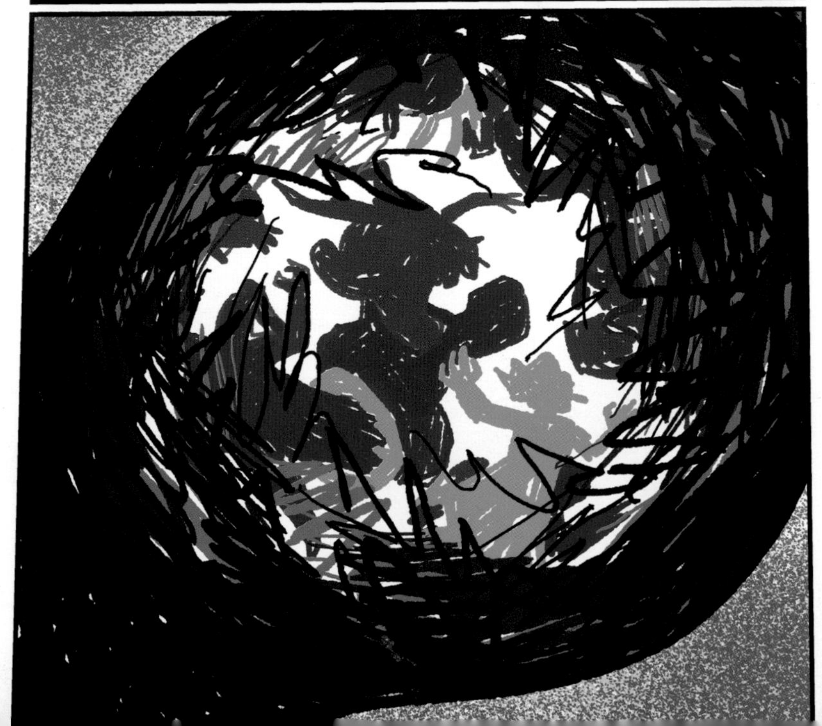

IS THAT... BRU'S MAGIC?
AND THE BUTTERFLY BRIGADE'S?
DREW, WHAT CAN WE DO?
HE ABSORBS WHATEVER HE EATS.
HE JUST GETS BIGGER AND MORE POWERFUL.

THAT'S **EXACTLY** WHAT HE'S DOING.
EATING WHATEVER WE THROW AT HIM...

BECK!
WHAT'VE **YOU** GOT?
ARE YOU READY?

WHAT? **ME**?
BUT... **LOOK** AT HIM!
CAN YOU HOLD HIM OFF?
JUST FOR A MINUTE?
I NEED...
I NEED **TIME**.

WHAT?
TIME FOR **WHAT**??

I HAVE IT!
FINALLY!
A PLAN!

OKAY.
OKAY.
BECK, AREN'T YOU **READY**?

YES! I JUST... **HERE**, DOODLES!

USE THE FORCE-FIELD GENERATORS TO HOLD HIM OFF!!

OKAY, THAT SHOULD BUY US SOME TIME.
LIKE, A FEW SECONDS?
DON'T PAY ATTENTION, DOODLES. YOU'RE DOING GREAT.
NOW HERE, HELP DINAH ASSEMBLE THE WARBOT!
ASSEMBLE IT?
YOU'RE STILL PUTTING STUFF TOGETHER?
IT WOULDN'T ALL FIT IN HERE, GEEZ!
WAIT, WARBOT? NO ONE TOLD ME ABOUT A WARBOT!!

QUICK, DINAH!
GET TO THE CONTROLS!
BEFORE HE BREAKS THROUGH!
CAN I HELP?
I WANNA **HELP**!
UMMM...

PAPRGHHHH

GRANDPA, LOOK!
LET'S HELP!
SURE! WHAT IS IT?

IT'S THE LEVERATHON!
A NEW ONE!
WHAT? A NEW ONE?
DREW, WHAT ARE YOU DOING!?
I'M DRAWING AS FAST AS I CAN!!!!

I DON'T KNOW IF THIS IS A GOOD IDEA, DREW...
DO YOU HAVE A **BETTER** ONE!?

I'M HELPING!
I CAN HELP!
UH...

MAYBE THIS CAN **WORK**?
LIKE... **LIGHT** VERSUS **DARK**?
RIGHT, RIGHT!

WHATEVER YOU'RE GONNA DO, YOU'D BETTER DO IT **SOON**!!!

HERE, EVERYONE!
GRAB A MARKER!
BUT...

HOW ELSE WILL YOU FINISH IN **TIME**, DREW?
YEAH, LET'S **DO** THIS!

AM I DRAWING HIS FINS RIGHT?
DOES HE **HAVE** FINS?

IT'S FINE!
IT'S **GREAT**.

I'M SO SORRY, DINAH, I DIDN'T THINK THIS THROUGH!
IF WE OVERCHARGE THE FLUX CAPACITORS,
MAYBE WE CAN SET THE WARBOT TO DETONATE?
WHAT ABOUT A WORMHOLE?
OR...
HEY!
LEVIATHAN!

EAT THIS!!!

ROAR!!

GRRRR

LICK

RR?
HSSSSS
C'MON...
RARRGHHH!!
eeeee!

RRRRRRRR
eeeeeeeeeeeee
RRRA
RRA
eeeeee
AAHH!!

THIS WAS YOUR PLAN?
THAT THEY'D **EAT** EACH OTHER?
UMMM...

GRRARGRRR
RRRRGGRARRRRGRSSRRRARARA
sssRRRRRGRRARG

WHAT HAPPENED?
IS IT OVER?

DREW, WHERE ARE YOU GOING?
BE CAREFUL!
WHO WON?

I...
UM...
I THINK...

I THINK IT'S GONNA BE OKAY.

WAIT, SO...
WHICH LEVIATHAN IS THIS ONE?
YEAH, DID THE NEW ONE EAT THE OLD ONE?
OR IS THIS... A WHOLE NEW CREATURE?
HI, LEVI!
UM...
LET'S JUST CALL HIM LEVI.

BUT...
WHAT HAPPENED TO ALL THE DOODLES?
YEAH, WHAT ABOUT DINAH AND CAPTAIN AND...
I DON'T **KNOW**. I WAS HOPING THAT...
UM...?
BLRGH

UM.
HURRAY?

HURRAY!!!!!

CHAPTER 11: A NEW DOODLEVILLE

I'VE MISSED ALL OF YOU SO, **SO MUCH**.

WELCOME **HOME**.

I'M REALLY GONNA MISS THE DOODLES.
YEAH, THEY'RE SO GREAT, DREW.
I'M GLAD WE GOT TO KNOW THEM BETTER.
HUH?
WHY DO YOU SOUND SO SAD?
YOU'RE TALKING AS IF YOU'RE NEVER GOING TO SEE THEM AGAIN.
YOU'RE THE ONES WHO SHOWED ME WHAT THE DOODLES CAN DO.
I NEVER WOULD HAVE KNOWN THAT THEY COULD BE... HEROES.
BUT...
NOW THAT WE'VE WON, DON'T YOU WANT THINGS TO GO BACK TO NORMAL?
NORMAL?
OF COURSE NOT! I WANT TO KEEP DOING AMAZING STUFF WITH ALL OF YOU!
...DON'T YOU WANT TO?

OF COURSE WE DO!
YEAH, WE'VE BARELY GOTTEN STARTED!
I LOVE YOU, ART CLUB!!!
UNITED!

SO, UM, WHAT'S NEXT FOR DOODLEVILLE?
YEAH, ARE YOU GONNA REBUILD EVERYTHING?
UM... I GUESS?
IT'S... A LOT.
ARE YOU GONNA MAKE IT THE SAME AS IT WAS?
OR DIFFERENT?
WHY?
...DO YOU HAVE SOME IDEAS?

HELLOOOO, ART CLUB!
WHAT DID EVERYONE... DO...THIS... WEEKEND?

UM, SOOO... WE SAVED THE LEVIATHAN AND STARTED BUILDING A NEW DOODLEVILLE.
WHAT!?
OR... A DOODLEVERSE?

BUT THERE'S NOT ENOUGH ROOM AT MY HOUSE, SO...
YOU SAVED THE--
YEAH, SO WE'RE EACH BUILDING OUR **OWN** CITIES.
OR CASTLES OR ACADEMIES OR WHATEVER.

YOU **WON**???
KIDS!!!!
I'M **SO** HAPPY!
YOU'RE ALL **INCREDIBLE**!

MR. SCHNEIDER, WE WANTED TO SHOW YOU WHAT WE'VE GOT. IS THAT OKAY?
OF COURSE! I CAN'T WAIT!

I PRESENT...
SCRIBBLE CITY!
IT'S PROUDLY PROTECTED BY CAPTAIN COCKATOO AND HIS COMMANDOS!
HERE'S THE DOWNTOWN...
HERE'S THE L STOP...
UNDERNEATH ALL THAT IS THE SECRET SUPERDOODLE HEADQUARTERS,
THEIR MEETING ROOM...
TRAINING ROOM...
AND OF COURSE A SUPERHERO HOT TUB.

THIS IS THE OCCULT ACADEMY, AND YES, IT'S BASICALLY A SCHOOL FOR WITCHES.
THEY CAN STUDY ALCHEMY, SHAPE-SHIFTING, CURSES...AND CURSE WORDS.
NO MAGIC IS FORBIDDEN AT THE OCCULT ACADEMY!
THEY HAVE A NICE BIG GATHERING HALL,
PLENTY OF BOOKS IN THE LIBRARY...
AND OBVIOUSLY...
EVERYONE GETS THEIR OWN PRIVATE DORM ROOM.

YOU REMEMBER THAT THE MAGICAL BUTTERFLY BOYFRIENDS ARE FROM TWO DIFFERENT KINGDOMS, RIGHT?
THIS IS THE **CLOUD KINGDOM**, HIGH IN THE SKY...
HERE'S THE **CATERPILLAR CASTLE** RIGHT IN THE MIDDLE, WHERE THE TWO PRINCES CAN LIVE TOGETHER.
THEY GUARD BOTH KINGDOMS FROM EVIL AND IGNORANCE...
BUT THEY **DO** TAKE ROMANTIC **VACATIONS** ONCE IN A WHILE.
DOWN HERE IS THE **BLOSSOM KINGDOM**.
IT SMELLS REALLY GOOD BECAUSE I USED SCENTED MARKERS.

IT'S FINALLY COMPLETE! MY **MASTERPIECE**!
THE D.A.R.E. SPACE STATION!
(DEEP ASTRONOMICAL RESEARCH AND EXPLORATION, IF THAT WASN'T OBVIOUS.)
IT'S GOT FULLY FUNCTIONAL ARTIFICIAL GRAVITY,
PLENTY OF PORTS FOR SPACESHIPS...
DEEP-SPACE SCANNERS...
RESEARCH LABS...
ALL KINDS OF PROTOTYPES...
AND THE ENTIRE STATION TRANSFORMS INTO A **GIANT WARBOT** IN CASE OF INTERSTELLAR EMERGENCIES!

SO, DREW...
WILL THE DOODLES STAY SPLIT UP LIKE THIS?
BECAUSE THAT SEEMS LIKE A SHAME.
NO, THEY CAN VISIT EACH OTHER WHENEVER THEY WANT!
THEY JUST TAKE THE L!
THE L?
YOU DREW AN ENTIRE **TRAIN SYSTEM**?
OH LOOK, THERE **ARE** LITTLE TRAIN STOPS, AREN'T THERE?
HERE HE COMES!
WHAT? **WHO**?
OMG.

AH! THE L!! I GET IT!
LEVI, IT'S SO GOOD TO SEE YOU!
I LOVE THE NEW LOOK!
THAT IS TOO COOL!
KIDS, CAN YOU MAKE AN L STOP FOR THE CLASSROOM?
PLEEEEASE?

LATER, AT THE DINER...
HI, RICKY! HOW'S YOUR DOODLE DINER?
IT'S OPEN FOR BUSINESS!
IT LOOKS GREAT!
THE ONLY THING IT'S MISSING...
IS A GOOFY GRANDPA SITTING AT THE COUNTER ALL THE TIME!
HEY!
HAHAHAHA!
AND GIVE HIM AN AWESOME MUSTACHE!
HA HA, YOU'D BETTER!

SO WHAT'S TODAY'S SPECIAL, RICKY?
UMMM... MEAT LOAF!
HA HA!
YOU KNOW, I THINK LEVI IS A VEGETARIAN.
EWW, VEGETABLES?
YUP!
...IS CHOCOLATE A VEGETABLE?
HAHAHA!

DREW?
YOU'RE STILL UP?
YEAH, I'M WORKING ON DOODLEVILLE.
I WANT TO MAKE IT PERFECT.
OR AT LEAST... BETTER.
AND I NEED TO MAKE LOTS OF SPACE FOR LEVI!
WELL... I'M SURE IT WILL BE GREAT.
YEAH, WE'RE SO PROUD OF YOU, SWEETHEART.
AND I CAN'T EVEN IMAGINE WHAT YOU'LL COME UP WITH NEXT!

DON'T STAY UP TOO LATE, OKAY?
I WON'T!
AND...
WAIT.
WHAT IS MIKE WEARING?
IS THAT A HAT?
DID YOU PAINT THAT?
UMMM...
HE... BORROWED IT?
BUT WE'RE BRINGING IT BACK.
SOON.
I SWEAR.

OKAY, LEVI...
WE'VE PRACTICED THIS A MILLION TIMES.

BRING THE HAT BACK TO THE BABY, THEN GET OUT OF THERE!

JUST STICK TO THE PLAN... AND WE'RE GOOD.

GOOD LUCK, LEVI!
COME RIGHT BACK TO MY NOTEBOOK WHEN YOU'RE DONE!
YOU!!!
YOU!?!?
AAAAHHHHHHHHH!!!!

PANT
PANT
DID YOU DO IT, LEVI?
DID YOU...?
UH

THIS WAS **NOT** THE **PLAN**!!!

TO BE CONTINUED . . .

ACKNOWLEDGMENTS

I'm eternally thankful to everyone who helped me in countless ways over the course of *Doodleville's* long journey. Although I can't possibly list everyone, I wanted to specifically thank:

My editor, Marisa DiNovis, for her endless support, enthusiasm, and unerring eye for detail. April Ward for her incredible art direction, and the entire Knopf team: Melanie Nolan, Josh Redlich, Brenda Conway, Janine Perez, Kristin Schulz, Jake Eldred, Nancy Siscoe, Artie Bennett, Alison Kolani, Emily DuVal, Nicole Valdez, Dawn Ryan, and Sylvia Bi.

My literary agent, Dan Lazar, for more than a decade of advice, advocacy, and encouragement.

Barbara Perez Marquez, Teo DuVall, Jasmine Walls, Deanna Arsala, Levi Hastings, David DeMeo, Michael Cole, Manuel Betancourt, Vid Alliger, Adam Guerino, Steve Foxe, Ingrid Law, and Mary Winn Heider, who gave crucially important feedback and encouragement.

The Art Institute of Chicago.

My parents, Tom and Pat.

My husband, Dan.

AUTHOR'S NOTE

Drawing can be magical.

I've been drawing my whole life, and it still feels like magic to me. Although my doodles don't dance across my walls or hide in priceless paintings, I'm able to bring them to life with my comics. After all, that's how I shared Drew's story with you in this very book!

Sometimes, though, drawing can be frustrating and a lot of work. It's taken me a long time to make *Doodleville.* Believe it or not, I first started working on this book more than ten years ago! And many of the characters you've met in *Doodleville* have been living in my head for even longer than that. (I'll share some more about them in the next few pages!)

I hope that reading this book inspires you to bring your *own* characters to life, whether in sketchbooks, in comics, or even on the walls of your home! (But maybe check with a grown-up first!)

And I hope that this book encourages you to *share* your characters and their stories, too! Art can connect us with each other. And it can communicate how we're really feeling. When you combine your creativity with the talents of others, you never know what might happen! My first graphic novel, *The Cardboard Kingdom,* was made with ten other writers. They helped me see my characters with fresh eyes, and they gave me the confidence to write and draw *Doodleville* by myself! Even when I doubted my abilities, they gave me the advice and the encouragement I needed to make this book.

Doubt is the enemy of every artist, young or old. It is what creates the Dark Leviathan and causes so much trouble for Drew and her friends. Draw fearlessly and don't fuss over flaws. Don't worry about erasing or crossing things out. Learn from your mistakes, but don't get *stuck* on them. The only way to get *better* at drawing is to *keep* drawing.

Like I said, I have spent ten years trying to tell Drew's story in *Doodleville.* Over the course of those years, I struggled with doubt and made mistakes, but I also learned a whole lot. Many friends helped me along the way by reading this book and sharing their feelings about it, whether good or bad. As I look back on it, ten years doesn't really seem so long, and every challenge along the way was a lesson I had to learn to make the book that you are holding in your hands right now.

In a way, Drew's story in *Doodleville* is a lot like my own—full of drawing and doubt and doodles. But it's just the start of *her* story! Drew's adventures will continue in Book 2 of the Doodleville series!

AN ANNOTATED HISTORY OF THE DOODLES

Some of the doodles that you've met in *Doodleville* can be found in the oldest sketchbooks from my own childhood! I went digging through dozens of those books to find their first few sketches and to share a little bit about how they've grown (or, in some cases, shrunk??) over the years!

PANJA

I first started drawing Panja when I was twelve or thirteen, and I haven't stopped drawing him since! He was originally going to be a ninja panda—that's where his name comes from! But over time, he's transformed into less of an action hero and more of an adorable little friend!

BILLY

I've been drawing Billy since I was a teenager. He's always been goofy and generous, expressive and innocent. I love the idea that a slug, which might be slimy and gross to some people, is actually a total sweetheart! No matter what, Billy tries to help his friends, even if he doesn't know how.

KITTYBUNNY

Kittybunny, a cute cat with floppy bunny ears, is the complete opposite of Billy the Slug—and she's got a dark side! In fact, you can see in this early sketch of her that I originally gave her demon horns instead of rabbit ears! But I don't think I meant to give her wheels—those circles were part of a different doodle! Oops!

MIKE

I've always thought of Mike as a big, friendly ogre. He's a little less fearsome nowadays than when he started out, though. Back then, he had bigger teeth and claws. At some point, he developed a fondness for hats, which was an unexpected (but delightful) surprise!

THE ART CLUB'S HEROES

CAPTAIN COCKATOO

I love superheroes, especially if they're based on silly animals. Much like Ameer, I had a bird as a pet when I was a kid. Though instead of his majestic pink cockatoo, I had an adorable little cockatiel!

(Yes, they're different kinds of birds!) Although I have drawn Captain Cockatoo in a lot of different ways over the years, my favorite part of drawing him has always been the tuft of feathers on top of his head because it is so funny, fluffy, and expressive!

DINAH DARE

I've always loved science fiction—whether I'm reading about space, or time travel, or futuristic technology! Dinah Dare is an inventor extraordinaire: anything you can think of, she can make it! But even though Dinah's gadgets are high-tech, I made them all really fun and easy to draw, often using simple shapes like circles and triangles.

BRU

I wanted each of the Art Club's characters to have a distinctive style, and with Bru, my design was all jagged angles and pointy bits—even that wand is crooked! When I was creating this character, I had someone in mind like Amethyst from *Steven Universe* meets Sam the Goblin from *The Cardboard Kingdom*!

THE MAGICAL BUTTERFLY BOYFRIENDS

The two princes were inspired by cartoons like *Sailor Moon*, which feature fabulous costumes, magical accessories, and lots of sparkles. Their magic is about connection, and they are more powerful when they are together. I like to think that real life is like that, too—that we're capable of achieving amazing things when we reach across our differences and connect with each other.

Many of the other doodles in this book are more recent creations, and they resulted from several long sessions of doodling and daydreaming just to see what would happen! Sometimes I would create a creature, and I wouldn't even know what they were supposed to be! That might seem strange, but it's what Drew does with her doodles, too. They rarely turn out the way she expected! The characters you draw today might grow and change alongside you all your life!

HOW TO DRAW A DOODLE

One of my favorite doodles to draw is Gloop. There's no wrong way to draw Gloop!

1. First, start with an eye—just a circle and a dot in the middle!

2. Second, draw another eye wherever you want.

3. His mouth looks kind of like a bean.

4. Give him two teeth!

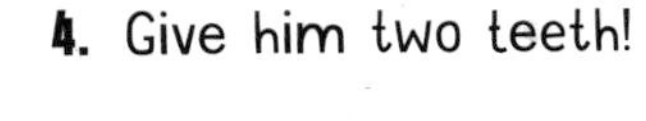

5. Now draw a circular shape for his head.

6. Draw some more squiggles for his body! There you go! That's Gloop!

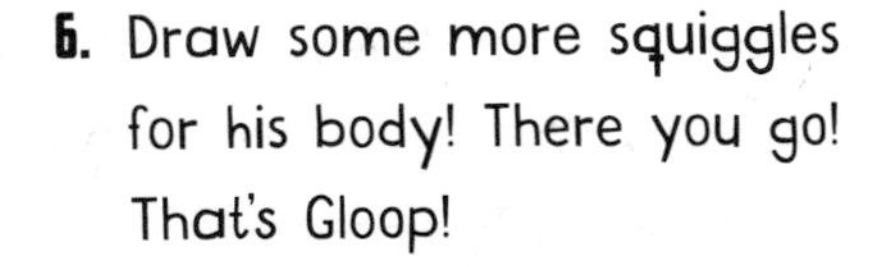

Doodleville **is dedicated to the arts educators who made me the artist that I am, and to those who continue teaching their students to make magic every day in their classrooms.**
—C.S.

THIS IS A BORZOI BOOK PUBLISHED BY ALFRED A. KNOPF

Visit us on the Web! rhcbooks.com

Educators and librarians, for a variety of teaching tools, visit us at RHTeachersLibrarians.com

Library of Congress Cataloging-in-Publication Data is available upon request.
ISBN 978-1-9848-9470-0 (trade) — ISBN 978-0-593-12682-0 (lib. bdg.) —
ISBN 978-1-9848-9472-4 (ebook) — ISBN 978-1-9848-9471-7 (trade pbk.)

The text of this book is set in Creative Block BB.
The illustrations were created using Clip Studio Paint.
Interior design by Chad Sell

MANUFACTURED IN CHINA
June 2020
10 9 8 7 6 5 4 3 2 1

First Edition